Sneaky Snacks

By
Jeremy Padgett

Illustrations
Penny Serrano

Book Design and Illustrations by Penny Serrano
Instagram:@pennys_wings

Story by Jeremy Padgett
www.jeremypadgett.com
Instagram: @ShutUpJeremy
Facebook: facebook.com/ShutUpJeremy

The text of this book was set in Farm New.
The illustrations were a combination of hand painted textures put together in Procreate and Photoshop.
ISBN: 9798507218547

Jeremy Padgett is a husband and father of two young energetic children who love books!

Jeremy is an award-winning morning radio personality, local influencer, writer and voice-over talent - located in Denver, Colorado. He adds an exceptional level of wit and sarcasm to the radio airwaves where many of his hilarious stories about raising his children can be heard all over the world.

Jeremy holds a Bachelor of Arts in Speech Communications and Broadcasting and also a Minor in Marketing from the Metropolitan State University of Denver - graduating with honors.

At the time of this writing, he has never had a cavity.

For Reid and Lyla
I'm sorry that I keep eating all of your
peanut butter cups.
-Dad

For my parents, sister and husband...
I'm not sorry for not sharing
my chocolate bars with you.
-Penny

My school day was over,
I was ready to snack.
I ran to my cubby and
grabbed my big pack.

I said goodbye to my
friends and so long to
my teacher.

My stomach
was growling
like a
big
scary
creature!

I needed
a pizza or
some chips
in my diet.

But as I arrived
home, it seemed
oddly quiet...

I crept down
the hall and
listened
real close.

Sniff
Sniff
Sniff
Sniff
Stuck my head
in the air
and sniffed
with my nose.

I snuck to the kitchen to find **my mom** in the act.

She was eating some candy out of a **big** grocery sack!

Gum
Gum
Gum

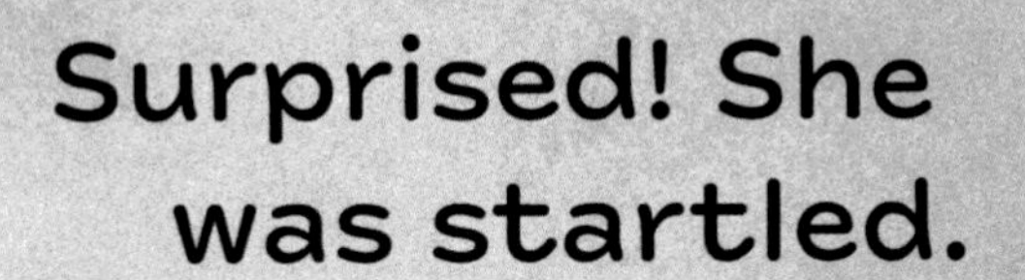

Surprised! She
was startled.

She chewed and
she swallowed.

She ran to the
cupboard and
I quickly
followed.

"Where have you been hiding that
chocolatey fare?"
"It's a secret" she said, and threw
her hands in the air!

"Now how about we get something nutritious to eat.

You're a growing young lady you need healthy, not sweet."

Bummed and bewildered
I rolled my big eyes.

Where has she been hiding that?
She knows I'm quite wise.

My mom and my dad
have all the great snacks.
They're gummy and chewy
and come in big packs.
They're cheesy and crunchy,
salty and gooey...

But mom says
NO treats.
Just veggies?
OH
PHOOEY!

I just want a soda or
a big slice of pie.

If I don't get brownies,
I'm just gonna cry!

They tell me
I'm growing
and sprouting
up tall.

I shouldn't be
crunching
on candy at all.

Enough of this
madness I need a good plan.
I must find some gummies
I'll do all that I can!

I’ll look under the pots
and under the pans...

behind the
big toaster...

and around
all the cans...

All of my favorite
delights have just
dissapeared.

I’m looking all over-
this is getting quite weird...

They're not in the
pantry with the rest
of our food.

Mom's hiding the
good stuff,
which is really
quite rude!

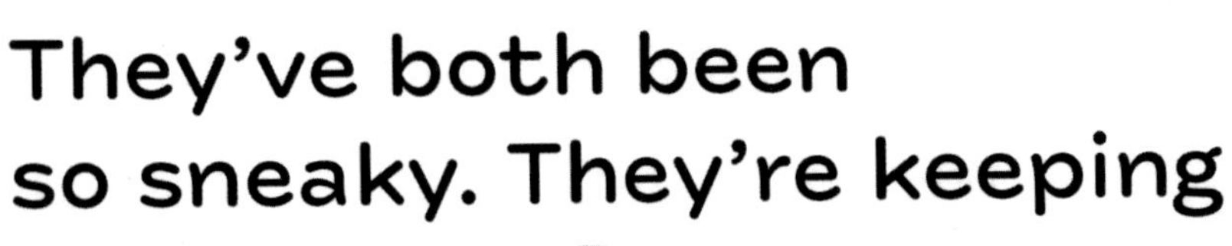

They've both been
so sneaky. They're keeping
a stash.

I hope they're not hiding
them way down
in the trash.

Instead of **BIG** muffins, I get apples galore.

I'm stuck with orange carrots. I can't take anymore.

I just want a nibble, a small little bite.

Oh, it would bring me such giddy delight!

I’m searching
up high...
and searching
down low.
But I can’t
find the sweets,
“Mom, where did
they go?”

She gives me a smile
and a quick little shrug.
And says with a laugh,
"Go check
under the rug!"

I know what to do
I'll form a big plan!

I'll find that whipped cream
and eat the whole can.

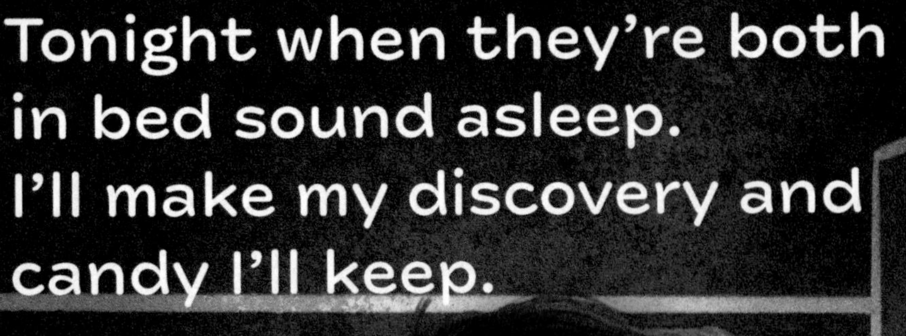

Tonight when they're both
in bed sound asleep.
I'll make my discovery and
candy I'll keep.

I'll sneak out of my room and search
the whole house.

I'll pat down the dog and talk to
our mouse.

The cookies and lollies
will all NOW be mine.

I'll fill up with
sugar and then
I'll feel fine!

I'll eat up some frosting
and toss out the grapes.

Fill up on licorice and
devour the crepes.

My parents will wake to find no treats in sight.

Nothing will be left.
Not even one bite.

The taffy and pretzels,
the marshmallows too.

All in my tummy
and none left
for you!

I will finally demolish their
chocolate bar stash.

I'll eat it all up
and then I will crash.

My tongue will
be sore from
this sweet
success.
Now to find someone
to pick up this mess!

Tomorrow,
I promise
I'll drink a
healthy green
shake.

But for right now.
I'm going to nap
on this
cake!

Made in the USA
Monee, IL
13 July 2021